Four Paws, Two Feet, ONE TEAM

Written by Connor Quinn and Mary Cortani

Illustrated by Susan Szecsi

For Jed Zillmer and all those veterans who lost the war at home.

Special thanks to Janice Madrid and everyone who contributed to making this book a reality.

C. Q.

To the dogs that rescue our veterans, to those that have supported OFP, and most importantly to my best boy, CJ, who continues to guide me.

M. C.

Hi, my name is Dakota,
and I'm a service dog.

I wasn't always a service dog. When I was just a pup, my brothers, sisters, and I were left out in a field. Something happened to our mother, and we were all alone. Then, a man found us.

He carried us home, fed us, and kept us warm. He saved us! But, he couldn't keep us.

Hello Mary...

Luckily, he had a friend who could help. She ran an organization called Operation Freedom Paws that saved dogs like us.

Operation Freedom Paws was to be our new home. And boy, were we happy! We made lots of new friends—some were dogs who had been rescued just like me. Some of them were humans, and they took care of us. Some of them loved to play with us.

Some liked to sing to us.

One of them liked to wrestle,

so I would always steal his hat!

Then, there is Mary. She's the one who started this place. She tells us we have a special purpose. She wants us to grow up to be service dogs. You see, Operation Freedom Paws doesn't just rescue dogs. They rescue people, too!

Mary teaches us that we are important dogs. We can sense the injuries people have that aren't noticeable on the outside.
And we do it with our NOSES.

Scientists say our sense of smell is about ten thousand times better than humans' sense of smell.

Secret Super Power

We can smell all kinds of different things, which means we can help all kinds of people.

For example, we can warn people when they need to take their medication, or when they need to rest.

We can help them feel safe
and cheer them up when they
start to feel stressed or sad.

That's why every dog at
Operation Freedom Paws trains
so hard. We have a job to do!

I used to dream every night about how I was going to make a difference in someone's life.

When the day finally came for me to meet my forever person, I was really nervous.

He looked so tough! I didn't think he needed anybody to help him.

He has something called Post Traumatic Stress Disorder. You see, my forever person is a war veteran. He fought in many battles far from home, and he came home with injuries. They are the type of injuries you can't see with your human eyes, but I can smell them with my nose! That's why Mary put us together.

When we first started training, it was hard, and he made some mistakes.

I had to teach him a whole bunch of things so I could help him when we go out into the world.

When we practice out in the world with other people, I always wear a vest that says, "WORKING DOG DO NOT PET!" That way, I can concentrate on him and not have to worry about distractions. There are always nice people who want to meet us, but they have to ask very politely if they can visit me. Sometimes, he says no, and nobody should feel bad about that. I'm a working dog, and I need to focus on my job.

It took us a while, but I finally earned my Operation Freedom Paws Service Dog Vest and became a certified Service Dog.

That's when my real work started.

When he took me home, I learned that he gets nightmares.

So, it is is my job to wake him up and let him know everything is okay.

That isn't the only problem, though.

He also gets really nervous in crowds. In the beginning, any time we would go into a large space with lots of people, my nose would go haywire!

One day, his daughter wanted to bring him to her school for show and tell.

My forever person really wanted to go, but that's just the type of place that makes him the most nervous.

We went back to train.
We had to work very hard
in order to be ready.

Here, we are doing puppy yoga. It makes everyone relaxed and helps us bond.

Mary and all the other service dogs and their forever persons at Operation Freedom Paws came and helped us out, because we're a family!

We finally got the confidence
to go out and face his fears.

As we walked into her school, I smelled his discomfort. I gave him a nudge with my nose. That always lets him know I'm there with him.

After a while, he was able to relax with me at his feet, and we waited for his daughter's turn at show and tell.

SERVICE DOG

And, surprise! I was the one she wanted to show.
My tail wagged very fast as she told the whole
class about how her dad and I work together.

I could smell how happy
my forever person was.
In fact, I could smell how
happy everyone was!

SERVICE DOG

32

It was the
greatest day ever!

PAWS FOR EFFECT

Emilio and Samson

You know when I need you,

And when I see you, I feel at ease,

And my heart feels warm,

And the storm of uncertainty and anger

No longer consumes me,

And it's easy to walk, and easy to talk

Without my burdens being more than I can bear,

And when I stare into your inviting eyes,

I realize that I'm not alone,

And I never will be,

And your wagging tail helps me see

Something new on the horizon,

Rising over the hills of despair,

And I don't care, that I'm not who I used to be,

Because I'm me,

And being me brought me to you.

by Emilio Gallegos

ABOUT THE AUTHORS AND ILLUSTRATOR

Connor Quinn is a veteran, having served nine years in the Army as a Combat Medic with two tours to Afghanistan. He holds an Associate's Degree in Spanish from Gavilan College and a Bachelor's degree in Health Science from San Jose State University. In 2018, he took a job as a kennel technician at Operation Freedom Paws. He became inspired to write *Four Paws, Two Feet, One Team* after witnessing the incredible transformation of the veterans and the dogs in the program.

Mary Cortani served in the U.S. Army from 1975-1984 as a Certified Army Master of Canine Education instructor with over forty years of experience as a dog trainer. She is the founder and executive director of Operation Freedom Paws in San Martin, California. Her work with Operation Freedom Paws has garnered a Top 10 CNN Hero Award, Central Coast Jefferson Award, and the love and admiration of everyone she has empowered to restore their freedom to live life.

Susan Szecsi is an award-winning illustrator and designer. She has worked with many publishing houses, including Scholastic, Inc., Chicago Review Press, Hunter House Publishers, and Stanford University Press. Susan grew up in a small town in Hungary and always had dogs to play with. Susan has two children and lives with her husband in the Bay Area, California. See her portfolio at www.brainmonsters.com.

"Love heals, especially when it's got a wet nose, four paws and a wagging tail."

Mary-ism #3

For more information visit www.operationfreedompaws.org

TYPES OF SERVICE DOGS

Emotional Support Dog

An Emotional Support Animal (ESA) is a pet that helps its owner by being a buddy and giving love. Emotional Support Animals are trained just like other home pets to live peacefully among humans without being a problem or a danger to others. The difference is that their owners get to keep an emotional support animal in apartments or houses, even when there is a "no pets" policy. Emotional Support Animals can travel by plane with the person who has a disability if they have the right paperwork and the animal gets along well with other people. Restaurants, stores, and government offices do not have to allow emotional support animals into their buildings.

Mobility Assistance Dogs

Mobility Assistance Dogs help people who need help balancing and moving around.

Skilled Companion Dogs

Skilled Companion Dogs help people with disabilities who have trouble reaching a light switch, picking up a dropped pencil, picking up dropped keys, opening a door, and much more.

Mobility Assistance Dogs and Skilled Companion Dogs both require a facilitator. A facilitator is usually a parent, spouse, or caregiver who handles and cares for the assistance dog. The facilitator encourages a strong bond between the person with the disability and the dog. The facilitator also trains the dog to do the special jobs that help the person with the disability.

TYPES OF SERVICE DOGS

Psychiatric Service Dogs

Psychiatric Service Dogs are trained to help people with disabilities in the way they learn or feel. Very often, these dogs can be taught by the person with disabilities and with help from a professional dog trainer. A doctor has to write a letter or prescription that says that the veteran needs a dog to help them with their medical condition.

Seizure or Medical Alert Dogs

Seizure or Medical Alert Dogs can sense a seizure or a medical problem and alert their human. They have a very special skill, and not all dogs can do this. The dog knows the difference between normal and abnormal in her human's physical state. The dog can let the human know when a seizure is coming or when the human needs to take medicine.

Therapy Dogs

A Therapy Dog is trained to provide affection and comfort to people, but it is not a service dog. This is a family pet that has been trained and certified as a Therapy Dog to visit hospitals, schools, and nursing homes and to visit with people who have learning difficulties or who are in stressful situations.

REQUIREMENTS OF SERVICE DOGS

AGE: All service dog programs are only open to dogs that are between eight to ten months old and up to three years old. Puppies can be used, but it takes longer to train a puppy. It might take up to two years before having a Certified Service Dog. Sometimes, an owner may need a replacement service dog.

HEALTH: A service dog should be maintained in the very best possible health. Before entering the training program, the dog must be examined by a veterinarian. The dog needs to be vaccinated against diseases and needs to receive medicine every month for heartworm, fleas, and ticks. The dog needs nutritious food so that his skin and coat stay healthy, which reduces the shedding of hair and dander. A dog's nails need to be trimmed frequently to maintain foot health and to reduce any damage caused by overgrown nails on public and private property.

BEHAVIOR: To undergo service dog training, the dog should not be fearful, aggressive, overly excited, or show a desire to chase small animals or other dogs. Dogs that have these characteristics are not suited to becoming service dogs.

TRAINING: Dogs require very basic training for manners, overexcitement, and exposure to public settings. After this Basic Obedience training, dogs receive specific training based on age, breed, type of program, and the needs of the individual. Training can last from six months to two years. After the training program is successfully completed, a Canine Good Citizen certification is given. Other certifications are given as the team progresses.

Mary with the prospective service dog puppy, Dakota.